T0195982

BEING FRIENDS
Is Going to Be Fun

A Spring Celebration To Remember

To order additional copies of this book, contact:
Xlibris
844-714-8691
www.Xlibris.com
Orders@Xlibris.com

ISBN:	Softcover	978-1-6641-5179-6
	EBook	978-1-6641-5178-9

Print information available on the last page

Rev. date: 01/14/2021

Being Friends Is Going to Be Fun

A Spring Celebration to Remember

WRITTEN BY:
Patricia Wesley Sills
Illustrated by: Gennel Marie Sollano

The huge old oak tree offered a branch to the flower fairy known as Tiny Tateam to rest on. Tiny Tateam's assignment was to paint the violet flower petals a beautiful purple color.

Her long light brown curls were tousled, and her hair looked windblown. She held her hair out of her eyes with a purple braided headband with ties that dangled down her back.

Tiny Tateam dressed in her favorite color of purples. Her beautiful brown eyes were always quick to notice what was happening around her. She stood up on the branch and fluttered her wings and loved the way her wings sparkled in the sunlight which made them seem magical.

It always amazed Tiny Tateam, that no matter how many flowers she painted; her purple paint bucket never got empty. She dipped her paint brush into the tiny paint bucket and began to paint the violets that were growing wild at the edge of the meadow. As she painted each petal, she sang happy songs. "To you my beautiful violet, I give you a purple delight. You'll have shades that are dark and some that are bright. Soon my friends will be here to help me paint. With lots of purple colors, they will help me finish what I can't."

Mother Nature was dressed in her blue dress and white apron with large pockets. She always had to empty her pockets at the end of each day. They held tiny treasures she collected throughout the day and today was no different. She had collected several treasures that morning. There was a tail feather from Ms. Robin, and a few amazing colorful rocks from the stream. She picked up a fallen nest that belonged to the tiny hummingbird.

She pushed her wire rim glasses up on her nose to read the long list she had to get done on her green clipboard. You could hear the click of her black pen as she prepared to check off something that was completed on her list. "I checked on the violets in the opening by the forest. Thank you Tiny Tateam for doing such a good job. No purple grass or leaves this time. Did you finish the violets in the meadow? Were you able to add more shades of purple to the flowers?"

“The violets have been beautiful this year. Leaving some violets unpainted was a great idea.” Mother Nature continued looking at her list while she waited for Tiny Tateam to answer.

“Thank you, replied Tiny Tateam. I must have skipped a few violets because I didn’t mean to leave some violets unpainted. I finished the meadow and I tried hard not to get paint on anything but the violets. Tiny Tateam was stirring her paint as she glanced at Mother Nature.

Mother Nature was looking at Zapper Dapper Leland now, but told Tiny Tateam, “The unpainted violets looked good and don’t go back and paint them. Let’s just see if anyone else will notice. OK?”

"Zapper Dapper Leland! How are your projects going? I know knocking pinecones down isn't interesting, but it must be done for new growth on the tree. I've seen Molly squirrel has been helping some. She is a good helper, but remember, she hid the pinecones under our porch, and we had to remove a huge pile of pinecones. She had so many pinecones she didn't know what to do with them all." Mother Nature chuckled as she remembered the incident.

With a pinecone zapper in his hand, Zapper Dapper Leland replied, "I have zapped down about a million pinecones! Well, maybe not that many, but it was a lot. I followed Molly squirrel one day to see where she was hiding pinecones. She put them in the old cave close to Gabby Hill. It's full of pinecones so she will have plenty of pine nuts this winter."

Molly squirrel peeked around the pine tree branch to see if Mother Nature was looking at her. She thought to herself as she picked a pine nut from the pinecone, "I collect so many pinecones because of all my cousins and friends who like to eat from my storehouse of pinecones every winter."

"Ok my little fairies, thank you for helping keep the world beautiful. I do need to move on to my pixies who have been helping this year. We have so many new flowers that I asked Pixie Presley and Pixie EJ to help with flower painting this year. I do hope they have been working and not playing around. Pixies do get distracted and fly off to chase butterflies." Mother Nature kept talking as she walked away.

Pixie Presley was known to chase butterflies. Her wild blond curly hair and her light skin were complementary. Normally she would keep her hair in a tight ponytail or braids. Today, however, she left it down and kept it back with a lavender headband.

Her shirt was pastel blue and her lavender skirt matched her headband. Her silky skirt floated into a large circle when she twirled around.

She turned to see herself in the reflection of the pool of water she found while she was chasing that beautiful green and blue butterfly. She flexed her pink wings to make them sparkle in the rays of sunlight. “Amazing!! I love my new clothes. They are going to be the so much fun to wear. My lavender shoes with blue laces are beautiful.” She heard someone calling her name.

“Pixie Presley, are you ok? I noticed you haven’t been painting.” Mother Nature called out.

“I’m over here Mother Nature. I saw a new color of butterfly and had to check it out. I’m coming!” Pixie Presley shouted back as she took one last peek at herself in the pool of water and flew off in the direction of Mother Nature’s voice.

“Now Pixie Presley, how are you going to finish your painting if you don’t stick with your job? It’s only for a little while and then we will have Spring Celebration. We must get done with all the painting. No chasing butterflies or anything till we get all our painting done.

Pixie Presley answered. “Yes mam. I understand. I do want to attend the Spring Celebration. I’ll get the rest of the painting done today. Pixie EJ is close to the Oliver tree. There’s a lot of new flowers there.

"Ok, dear! I'll check back with you in a few hours. Do good and I'll check on Pixie EJ.

Mother Nature headed towards the Oliver tree. "Hello, Pixie EJ. I hope you have been busy." Mother Nature looked around to see what had been painted.

"Oh yes! I've been painting a lot. See!" Pixie EJ moved closer to Mother Nature and waited for her approval.

Pixie EJ's skin was dotted with pink smudges of paint. Her blue jumpsuit was smeared with pink paint. Even her blue shoes had pink smudges on them. Even her long brown hair had smudges of paint.

Her pixie wings were gold and glittered in the sunlight. She did have larger wings than regular pixie wings. It helped her to fly fast and do acrobats in the sky. Her abilities to do tricks and fly fast put her in a competing role with other pixies and some fairies, which she won the races most of the time.

"Oh my! You have been busy!" Mother Nature looked across the field around the Oliver tree. Every plant was now Peony Pink. She couldn't tell the flowers from the grass. The bushes were painted pink. "We have a misunderstanding of what you were to paint. The peony flowers are supposed to be pink. The grass is to be left green, as well as the bushes."

"Uh-oh! Now what? I loved the pink color and I thought it would be fun to see everything pink. I'm sorry! I don't know what to do to fix it." A little tear ran down Pixie EJ's cheek. Her lips quivered and her nose scrunched up a bit.

"Now, now my dear, let's see what we can do to fix this. Don't cry as you'll make me cry. Now won't that be a sight? The two of us crying in the woods." Mother Nature moved closer to Pixie EJ to comfort her with a hug and assure her things will be ok.

Pixie EJ lifted her face to Mother Nature and asked. "Do you have green paint? I could paint the leaves and grass green and fix this mistake. Can we do that?"

"Oh, my goodness! That's a terrific idea! You can paint the grass and leaves green again? That can be your job for the rest of the day. Mother Nature said as she reached into her shoulder bag. "Here's some green paint and brushes and you can make things right again."

"I can't wait to get started with my favorite color! It's going to be fun. I can do this job right. No pink grass here!" Pixie EJ started painting the blades of grass. With one swish of the brush and the blades of grass were green again.

The peony flower leaves took a little more time. Pixie EJ wanted to make sure no green paint got on the flower petals.

Mother Nature watched her pixie for a little while and called out, "I'm going to see how Pixie Presley is doing and I'll check back with you in just a little while."

Pixie EJ waved her hand to Mother Nature. Unluckily, it was the hand with the brush, and she plopped green paint in her hair. Just a small splat of green paint in a few places. Shrugging her shoulders, she didn't care if she had paint in her hair., She continued to paint her grass and the leaves on bushes.

Mother Nature could see the little pixie painting her yellow daffodils. She noted that it was only the flower petals that were painted yellow. Mother Nature took a deep sigh of relief.

Pixie Presley stopped painting when she saw Mother Nature coming. "Hey! I got all the flowers done since you left. I haven't seen any more butterflies. I'm almost done with this area, do you have more flowers for me to paint?"

"I sure do!" Replied Mother Nature. " There are a group of flowers on the hill across the Yellow meadow. It's north of the Oliver tree. You can't miss it as you will see the meadow is filled with yellow flowers. Just past the meadow is a hill that need flowers painted. I thank you for being so dependable. Our flowers need to be painted soon. It's their time!" Mother Nature sat on a tree stump. She smiled at Pixie Presley as she checked her list on her green clipboard.

After resting for a few minutes, Mother Nature decided to visit with Zapper Dapper Leland to see how his pinecone zapping was coming along. She stopped walking and could see he was zapping pinecones quickly off the tall pine trees. She watched for a few minutes until she saw he was trying to zap the squirrels. "What was Zapper Dapper Leland up too? He never hurts forest animals. Squirrels were hopping everywhere. "Zapper Dapper Leland! What are you doing?" She shouted and Zapper Dapper Leland stop zapping immediately.

Zapper Dapper Leland backed up and looked at Mother Nature. She had her hands on her hips and he hasn't seen her mad before. "I can explain! The squirrels were helping me move the pinecones and then stopped helping with everything, after I accidently zapped a squirrel and he jumped so high and fast. It was the funniest thing I have ever seen. I really didn't mean to zap him, but then the other squirrels started throwing pinecones at me. It hurt and I tried to protect myself."

Mother Nature's face softened, and she removed her hands from her hips. "Zapper Dapper Leland, no matter how it happened, you know we never hurt our forest friends. It sounds like it was an accident, but you handled it wrong. What is another way you could have handled it?"

"I could have said I was sorry. I shouldn't have laughed even if it was funny. It just blurted out. I didn't plan to laugh. I think that's why they got mad at me. I made a mistake," Zapper Dapper Leland explained the best he could. His voice lowered to a whisper she could hardly hear. "I am so sorry!"

Mother Nature looked behind Zapper Dapper Leland at the fifteen squirrels lined up on the lower pine tree limbs. Each had a pinecone in their hands. It looked like they were going to bomb him. They had listened to Zapper Dapper Leland's apology and dropped their pinecones. She noticed one of the squirrels was extra fuzzy and its tail was extremely bushy and figured that it must be the one that was zapped.

Mother Nature nodded her head at Zapper Dapper Leland in the direction of the squirrels. Zapper Dapper Leland turned around to see what she nodded at and jumped back closer to Mother Nature.

Zapper Dapper Leland yelled, "What's happening?"

Mother Nature said, "It's ok, they know you didn't mean to zap him, and they accepted your apology this time. They won't throw pinecones at you anymore. They may even help you if you ask them."

"I am sorry, and I could use your help if you would help me." Zapper Dapper Leland asked his furry friends.

Mother Nature smiled and nodded at the squirrels, "Great! I knew this could end well. Thank you my friends and you too, Zapper Dapper Leland for making this right. We need our forest friends. I'm going to see what Tiny Tateam's been up to. Keep up the good work." Mother Nature continued her journey as she checked her list on her green clipboard.

Tiny Tateam had been busy painting violets all day and was tired. "I must have painted a million violets today. That has to be a record." She watched the momma deer and her two little babies move around in the field looking for something to nibble on. She continued painting the flower petals.

Mother Nature looked at the momma deer and her babies. Something was different about them. They had purple smudges around their mouth. "What happened to the deer's mouth. It looks like they have been eating your freshly painted violets. Did you see them eat the violets?" She asked Tiny Tateam.

"I saw the deer but not their purple mouths. I was too busy painting the violets. I can't believe they ate so many of my painted violets. Will they get sick from the paint?" Tiny Tateam asked in a panic.

Mother Nature was still watching the deer and answered Tiny Tateam. "No, the paint is made with fairy dust and colors. It won't hurt them at all. I'm just not sure how long their mouths will be purple. You know flowers last a complete season. My oh my, this has never happened before in all my years. I must go tell them to stop eating till the flowers are dry They must have been following you all day."

While Mother Nature talked to mother deer and fawn, Tiny Tateam continued her painting in hopes to stay ahead of the deer. “I painted all those violets and they ate my hard work. I wished they could have waited till I didn’t see them eat my flowers. My arms are tired from painting all those violets. Really! Mother deer, couldn’t you have eaten the white ones, so I didn’t have so many to paint?”

Mother Nature explained to Mother deer and her fawn why they had purple mouths. The deer agreed to eat violets another day and bounced off on their way.

Mother Nature complemented Tiny Tateam for not getting mad at the deer and chasing them away. “The deer may have ran away never knowing why their mouths are purple and think something bad was wrong. Now they know and agreed to tell the other deer in the forest. That problem was solved quickly. You did a lot of work. They ate up several flowers and that is unfortunate, but the deer was doing what deer do. Eat beautiful and sweet violets.”

Tiny Tateam made a huffy sound as she finished the last of the violets and set down her bucket and brush. “Well, that’s done for here. Could we talk about the Spring Celebration?”

“Why yes! Said Mother Nature. I would like to talk to you about it right now. We are going to have it at the old oak tree in the meadow. The place we normally have our parties. I wanted to ask you if you if this Saturday would be a good day?” Mother Nature looked at her green clip board and made a note about the deer and their purple mouths.

Tiny Tateam was jumping up and down while clapping her hands. “Yes, oh yes! That is a great day. Everyone will be so excited to know we’ll have our Spring Celebration. I’ll tell everyone I see.”

"Everyone has been working so hard on their spring projects. I think a celebration would be great. Let's spread the word for anyone who wants to come on Saturday. They can bring a treat of their choice. I'll provide some flower nectar for drink. Tiny Tateam, it's going to be so much fun. Now you go tell your friends and I'll head back to home. Let me know how it's coming along!"

Tiny Tateam did what she was told. She told everyone she saw. "Spring Celebration this Saturday. Come to the old oak tree in the meadow. Bring a treat you will share with others and put on your dancing shoes. We are going to party all day!"

She told old fairies and young fairies. She told all the pixies she could find. She even told some blue birds that were teaching their young babies to fly. "It's going to be a wonderful day!"

Saturday came and everyone was gathering around the old oak tree. Some fairies brought some honeycomb the bees offered them to bring. Some pixies brought baked flower petals that tasted like candy but better. Some treats looked like fancy puddings and cakes. Everything just looked delicious.

Mother Nature brought a gallon of homemade flower nectar and tiny glasses to drink from. She commented that, "I hope this gallon will be enough! I had no idea there were so many fairies and pixies in the forest. There were pink, blue, green, white, brown, black and many more colors of new friends. Some were big and some were small. Some had big wings and there were some with no wings at all."

Mother Nature complemented Tiny Tateam, “You did a wonderful job on telling everyone. There have never been so many friends gathered laughing and dancing. We are going to have lots of fun with our new friends!”

Tiny Tateam told Mother Nature as she flew up beside her. “Amazing! I did tell everyone to bring a friend if they wanted. I guess they wanted to.”

“I hope we can be better friends with the new fairies and pixies. I can always use more help for the changing of the seasons. You have done the best of inviting people than anyone has ever done. Tiny Tateam, you did great!” Mother Nature leaned in toward Tiny Tateam and gave her a tiny kiss on her tiny cheek.

Tiny Tateam gave Mother Nature a tiny kiss on her cheek and told her, “Thank you. Now, let’s go dance around the oak tree.”

They joined hands in the circle of fairies and pixies and danced around the old oak tree till dark.

Spring Ce

oration

Printed in the United States
By Bookmasters